DATE DUE			
APR 6 01			
NOV 21 03			

3503 30007000264753

E
R
Recknagel,
Friedrich.

Meg's wish

This book was donated by
The Ferguson Family
in memory of

Mary Post,

a librarian at Russell Library who loved
books and children.

Copyright © 1999 by Nord-Süd Verlag AG, Gossau Zürich, Switzerland
First published in Switzerland under the title *Mia findet eine Freundin*
English translation copyright © 1999 by North-South Books Inc.

All rights reserved.
No part of this book may be reproduced or utilized in any form
or by any means, electronic or mechanical, including photocopying,
recording, or any information storage and retrieval system,
without permission in writing from the publisher.

First published in the United States, Great Britain, Canada,
Australia, and New Zealand in 1999 by North-South Books,
an imprint of Nord-Süd Verlag AG, Gossau Zürich, Switzerland.

Distributed in the United States by North-South Books Inc., New York.

Library of Congress Cataloging-in-Publication Data is available.
A CIP catalogue record for this book is available from The British Library.

ISBN 0-7358-1116-4 (trade binding)
1 3 5 7 9 TB 10 8 6 4 2
ISBN 0-7358-1117-2 (library binding)
1 3 5 7 9 LB 10 8 6 4 2
Printed in Belgium

For more information about our books,
and the authors and artists who create them,
visit our web site: http://www.northsouth.com

Friedrich Recknagel

Meg's Wish

ILLUSTRATED BY
Ilse van Garderen

Translated by Sibylle Kazeroid

North-South Books
New York / London

Meg and her parents had just moved to the city. In the
village where they used to live, everyone knew everyone
else. But here in the city, Meg didn't know anyone.

The children at the playground paid no attention to Meg.
They played and skipped around; sometimes they fought,
and then they played some more.

Meg watched them sadly.

At school too Meg kept to herself. She had seen most of
her classmates at the playground. Some of them even lived
in her apartment building—like Tina, who wore her hair
in a thick braid.

But Tina seemed to have
lots of friends already.

One night when her mother was tucking her in, Meg said, "If only I had a friend!" She had to swallow hard to keep from crying.

Mother stroked her hair. "We've been here only a week. You have to be patient." And to comfort Meg, she said, "It's August. And in August there are lots of shooting stars. If you see one, before it burns out, make a wish. Then it will come true."

When her mother left, Meg went to the window to look at
the sky, but she didn't see any shooting stars. It was cloudy,
and only the moon peeked through the clouds now and
then. Meg imagined that the moon was smiling. I'll try
again tomorrow, she thought, and went back to bed.

The next day was Sunday. "I would really like to see a
shooting star," Meg told her father.
"Hmm," mumbled Daddy.
A little later he said, "You know what? Tonight we'll drive
into the countryside. When it's very dark, maybe we'll be
lucky enough to see a shooting star."

At twilight they drove off in the car. When they were out
of the city, Daddy turned onto a dirt road and stopped.

"This is a good spot," Daddy said. "We'll wait here, and we'll build a little fire so that the wait will be more interesting."

Meg thought that was a great idea.

Soon a small fire was flickering. And Daddy had another surprise for her: he brought sandwiches and a thermos of tea from the car. They settled in next to the fire. Meg hadn't felt so happy in a long time.

It got darker and darker. First the big stars came out, then the small ones. Finally the sky was completely dotted with stars. Meg stared in amazement. But there wasn't a single shooting star. Daddy pointed to a bright star that was almost directly above them. "That's the North Star," he said. Then he showed her the Great Bear and the Little Dipper.

After a while Meg began to yawn. Then Daddy said, "I think it's time to go home. Don't be sad. You have to be patient with shooting stars."

I'll stand on the balcony every night until I get my wish, thought Meg.

But the next few days were cool and rainy. Big clouds covered the stars. Meg had to wait.

One night the sky was clear again. The full, round moon was smiling. Meg stood on the balcony and looked up. Suddenly a trail blazed across the sky.

"A shooting star!" cried Meg excitedly. "I wish . . ." But the shooting star had already burned out.

That night Meg crawled into bed, disappointed. She lay awake for a long time thinking about the children at the playground, especially Tina with the thick braid.

Suddenly it was strangely light in her room. The bed looked like a cloud. Meg got up. She felt very light, as if she were floating.

The balcony door opened by itself, and all at once Meg found herself in the exact spot where she and Daddy had sat beside the fire.

The sky was dotted with twinkling stars just as it had been before. Meg knew that her shooting star would come. It would be big and would shine a long time—long enough for her to make her wish.

Then there was a gleam of light over her, brighter and bigger than all the other stars—a shooting star, moving across the sky with its shining tail!

And Meg said solemnly, "I wish I had a friend."

As soon as she had said it, the shooting star went out.

The next day at breakfast Meg said, "I saw a shooting star in my dream and I made my wish."

"Then your wish will certainly come true," said Daddy.

"Really? But I only dreamed it!" said Meg.

"You'll see," Daddy replied.

Suddenly Meg was in a hurry. She grabbed her teddy bear and raced outside.

Tina was there. Meg went up to her.
Meg smiled, and Tina smiled back.
"Hi," said Meg.
"Hi," said Tina. "I like your bear."
"You can hold him if you want," said Meg, handing
the bear to Tina.
Tina stroked the bear's soft fur. "He's nice," she
said. "Come on. Let's play on the swings."

And Meg and her new friend raced off together
to the playground.